Thoughts: All that I am...

Thoughts, Volume 1

Lebohang Xavier Poetry and Lebohang Phoshuli

Published by Lebohang Xavier Poetry, 2024.

THOUGHTS: ALL THAT I AM...

First edition. March 2, 2024.

ISBN: 979-8224939961

Written by Lebohang Xavier Poetry and Lebohang Phoshuli.

Also by Lebohang Xavier Poetry

Mohlolo
Mohlolo: In the Shadows of Hope

Thoughts
Thoughts: All that I am...

Standalone
Mohlolo : In the shadows of hope.
Mohlolo: In the Shadows of hope.
Falling

Also by Lebohang Phoshuli

Mohlolo
Mohlolo: In the Shadows of Hope

Thoughts
Thoughts: All that I am...

Standalone
Falling

Table of Contents

Mpho Givenness Phoshuli

Moipone Anna Tsoai

Pontsho Khati

Preface

In the pages that follow, I invite you to join me on a reflective journey, a narrative woven with the threads of growth, seeking, and the intricate dance of identity. This is not merely a collection of chapters but a symphony of emotions that have shaped who I am today.

As I unveil my story, I challenge preconceived notions, navigating the shadows of hidden struggles, the echoes of familiar battles, and the unraveling of love. It's a journey through the strength within, the passions ignited by school, the trust deconstructed in fake friendships, and the price paid for authenticity.

Each chapter is a step in revealing the layers of stereotypes and unmasking the true identity that lies beyond labels. This is not just a book; it's an exploration of the human experience—the highs, the lows, and the intricate tapestry that makes us who we are.

So, as you embark on this voyage through the pages of "All That I Am," I invite you to feel deeply, reflect sincerely, and, perhaps, find echoes of your own story within these words.

1

2

Chapter 1: A Journey Unveiled

In the hushed moments before the journey commenced, a poignant reflection lingered in the air. The day they spirited me away from the comforting haven of my mother's home to the bustling streets of Pretoria is etched in my memory. Anticipation hung heavy, a blend of excitement and trepidation weaving through the air as we embarked on a journey that would shape the chapters of my life.

The journey transcended mere physical relocation; it marked a shift in the very essence of my existence. Leaving behind the warm embrace of my mother, I stepped into the unknown—Pretoria, a city with its own rhythm, its heartbeat pulsating with the cadence of blood pressure echoing an end to an era unexplored.

This departure was not just from the physical embrace of my mother but also from the familiar sounds of our home. The echoes of laughter, the shared stories, the songs that lulled me to sleep—all remained behind as we traversed the miles to Pretoria. The streets, once unfamiliar, became the backdrop of my early years—a multi-racial preschool where diversity thrived, where English became a language of solace.

Amid the whirlwind of new experiences, my grandmother's workplace emerged as a second home. Here, English became more than just words; it became a sanctuary where connections blossomed. Little did I know, these early bonds would be the threads connecting my past to my present.

Yet, within the walls of this new life, a shadow loomed. Michael, the boyfriend of my grandmother Albertina, cast a dark pall over our home. His actions were a discordant melody that reverberated through the walls, foretelling the challenges that lay ahead.

The news of Albertina's passing marked a somber return to the Free State. The comfort of English gave way to the challenge of Sesotho, and the swings of KHOTSO Primary School beckoned—a place where friendships seemed distant, and the language barrier became a formidable foe.

In the halls of Grade R, where established circles whispered stories of shared laughter, I stood on the periphery, a solitary figure yearning to weave my narrative into the fabric of their camaraderie. The game of holding hands in a circle became a metaphor for the challenges ahead—hands reaching out to form connections, yet mine left hanging in the air.

Grade 1 unfolded with its own set of trials, a grieving heart seeking solace in unfamiliar surroundings. The faces of Albertina, Giveness, Michael, and the compassionate Mrs. Bolara became anchors in a sea of uncertainties.

This chapter unfurls not only the physical journey but also the emotional landscape, a canvas painted with hues of anticipation, loss, and the yearning for connection. As I pen down these words, the echoes of that departure day still reverberate—a symphony of emotions that set the stage for the chapters yet to unfold.

Chapter 2: Connections

In the journey of my life, the Free State became more than just a geographical location; it became a canvas upon which my experiences were painted. As I navigated the twists and turns of growing up, friendship emerged as a central theme, shaping my understanding of camaraderie and support.

My friend, a constant companion in the chapters of my life, played a pivotal role in this narrative. From shared experiences to mutual growth, our friendship became a beacon of light in the sometimes tumultuous journey.

Growing up in the Free State offered a stark contrast to the bustling energy of Pretoria. It was a place where I envisioned becoming a stronger version of myself. The initial challenges of adapting to a new environment and overcoming language barriers were mere preludes to the complexities that awaited me.

The dynamics of KHOTSO, the school where I continued my primary education, provided both solace and challenges. The familiar pattern of swings and established friendship circles remained elusive, making the quest for companionship a formidable task. The echoes of bullying from my past followed me, creating a cloud of apprehension in my attempts to form connections.

Amidst the trials, my friend emerged as a steadfast ally. In the intricate dance of childhood friendships, we shared laughter, tears, and the unspoken language of companionship. Together, we faced the rigors of adapting to navigating the expectations of friendship circles, and confronting the lingering shadows of bullying.

The kaleidoscope of experiences in primary school revealed the resilience embedded in youthful connections. The fights, the reconciliations, and the shared moments of joy wove a tapestry of camaraderie that became an enduring part of my story.

As I reflect on the challenges of forming friendships in a new environment, it becomes evident that the bonds forged in those early years laid the foundation for the person I am today. My friend, a confidant and supporter, remains an integral part of the chapters yet to unfold.

Embedded within the fabric of my childhood, my mother's influence threaded through the tapestry of my early years in the Free State. The decision to live with my grandmother marked a departure from the daily presence of my mother, yet her impact lingered, shaping the contours of my formative experiences.

As I navigated the terrain of primary school, my mother's teachings reverberated, offering guidance in the intricate dance of adolescence. The sacrifices she made for my education and the unwavering love she bestowed from a distance became poignant markers of her enduring commitment.

The Free State, with its vast landscapes and unfamiliar faces, served as a backdrop for the evolution of our mother-son relationship. The geographical separation, a consequence of circumstances, fueled reflections on what might have been had I grown up in the constant presence of my mother.

In the quiet moments of contemplation, I found solace in the lessons she imparted. Her emphasis on resilience, kindness, and the pursuit of dreams became the foundation upon which I built my aspirations. The challenges of adapting to a new environment were met with the enduring strength derived from her teachings.

The dichotomy of physical distance and emotional closeness defined our relationship, making each day with her an important one, I was tasked to catch up on lost connection with her, and as I pen this thoughts down, I ask my self what would have been of me if I was without her, disastrous.

Amidst the complexities of adolescence, my mother's wisdom echoed in my ears, offering reassurance in moments of self-doubt. Her belief in my potential fueled my pursuit of education and self-discovery, instilling in me the confidence to navigate the challenges that lay ahead.

In the labyrinth of growing up, the maternal threads wove through the narratives of friendships and personal exploration. As I formed connections with peers and faced the trials of primary school, her influence remained a constant, an invisible force shaping my responses to the world.

The Free State, with its unique blend of experiences, became a crucible where the essence of maternal love and guidance melded with the journey of self-discovery. The unfolding chapters of my life bore the imprints of her wisdom, resilience, and unwavering support, creating a narrative that celebrated the profound impact of a mother's influence.

The dichotomy of physical distance and emotional closeness defined our relationship, making each day with her important. I found myself catching up on lost connections with her. As I pen down these thoughts, I reflect on what would have become of me without her – a disastrous scenario that I shudder to imagine. The complexities of adolescence were met with the enduring strength derived from her teachings.

IN THE LABYRINTH OF growing up, my mother's wisdom echoed in my ears, offering reassurance in moments of self-doubt. Her belief in my potential fueled my pursuit of education and self-discovery, instilling in me the confidence to navigate the challenges that lay ahead. As I formed connections with peers and faced the trials of primary school, her influence remained a constant, an invisible force shaping my responses to the world.

THE FREE STATE, WITH its unique blend of experiences, became a crucible where the essence of maternal love and guidance melded with the journey of self-discovery. The unfolding chapters of my life bore the imprints of her wisdom, resilience, and unwavering support, creating a narrative that celebrated the profound impact of a mother's influence.

As friendships blossomed and challenges unfolded, the chorus of friendship and maternal ties harmonized to create a symphony of support. The insecurities of adolescence were met with a reassuring melody of maternal advice, a melodic reminder of the unconditional love that anchored me in times of uncertainty.

THE EDUCATIONAL LANDSCAPE posed its own challenges, yet my mother's unwavering commitment to my academic pursuits became the guiding star. From early education in primary school to the intricate dance of friendships, her influence permeated every facet of my existence. The sacrifices made for my education became emblematic of a mother's enduring love.

The geographical separation from my mother, a consequence of circumstances, became a canvas upon which reflections of what might have been unfolded. The quiet moments of contemplation were accompanied by a profound sense of gratitude for the sacrifices she made. Her love, transcending physical distances, became a source of strength in the tapestry of my formative years.

The journey of self-discovery, intricately woven into the fabric of adolescence, echoed with the teachings of my mother. Her emphasis on resilience, kindness, and the pursuit of dreams reverberated as I navigated the complexities of growing up. Each step forward was guided by the wisdom instilled during those moments of maternal connection.

As I reflected on the maternal tapestry woven into the symphony of my life, the threads of guidance, sacrifice, and love became increasingly evident. The influence of my mother shaped not only my responses to the challenges of growing up but also the values and principles that underpinned my journey.

IN CONCLUDING THIS chapter, I am reminded of the privilege of having a mother whose impact transcends the physical boundaries that separated us. The Free State, with all its challenges and triumphs, became a canvas upon which the profound influence of maternal love and guidance painted the chapters of my adolescence. As I continue to navigate the journey of life, I carry with me the imprints of a mother's wisdom, resilience, and unconditional love – a guiding force in the symphony of my existence.

Chapter 3: Dead branch

Within the complexity of family structures, we often learn about complete family trees, including parents, siblings, cousins, and more. School lessons break down the biological processes, explaining how reproduction unfolds, from the movement of sperm to the fallopian tubes. However, in this chapter, we explore the real story of my family tree—a story marked by the absence of a key figure, my father. While the branches of my family tree may appear complete, the absence of my father creates gaps, leaving untold stories and unexplored connections. to offspring.

A family tree, a complex network of branches and connections, symbolizes the intricate relationships that mold our lives. Yet, within this intricate design, there lies a conspicuous absence—a branch that should be there but isn't. In the journey of my life, this absent branch takes the form of my father, an elusive figure whose physical presence did little to bridge the emotional gap.

The narrative unfolds in the context of a complete family tree, where both parents play integral roles. However, my experience diverges from this conventional structure. The separation of my parents at a young age marked the beginning of a familial landscape shaped by absence, and my father became the void in the family tree.

As I navigated the early years of life, the understanding of family dynamics was colored by the stark contrast between the theoretical teachings of school and the lived reality. The absent branch, my father, loomed as a persistent reminder of what could have been—a stable, two-parent household. The societal narratives of paternal involvement clashed with the reality of his sporadic presence.

The impact of this absence reverberated in various aspects of my upbringing. The void left by my father's absence seemed insurmountable at times, overshadowing the nurturing efforts of my mother. The emotional wounds, concealed beneath the surface, shaped my perceptions of self-worth and belonging.

It wasn't just the physical absence; it was the emotional disconnect that cut deeper. Instances where he was physically present but emotionally distant created a dissonance that lingered. The struggle to comprehend why a father could be physically there yet emotionally absent became a recurring theme in the family narrative.

The complexities intensified as I sought to build a relationship with my father. The yearning for a fatherly figure clashed with the harsh realities of rejection and indifference. Attempts to connect were met with resistance, leaving an indelible mark on the canvas of familial relationships.

The scars of rejection manifested in various incidents, each leaving an imprint on the evolving understanding of fatherhood. From being turned away when seeking solace at his home to enduring harsh words and criticism, the absent branch became a source of pain rather than support.

Despite these challenges, there were fleeting moments of hope—brief interludes where efforts to bridge the gap were met with a semblance of acknowledgment. However, these instances were transient, fading away as quickly as they appeared, leaving me grappling with a sense of unresolved longing.

In exploring the impact of this absent branch, the emotional landscape became a terrain fraught with complexities. The father-shaped void in the family tree cast shadows that extended into my perceptions of self, relationships, and the world at large. The absent branch wasn't just a familial void; it was a compass that guided my quest for identity and belonging.

The narrative takes a poignant turn as I recount instances of reaching out, hoping for a connection that transcended the physical and ventured into the realm of emotional support. However, the response, or lack thereof, solidified the realization that the absent branch was not just physically missing; it was emotionally vacant.

The absence of a fatherly presence also echoed in societal expectations and cultural narratives. The quest for self-identity became intertwined with the complexities of navigating a world that often idealizes the nuclear family structure. The absent branch became a counter-narrative, challenging societal norms and forcing a reevaluation of conventional definitions of family.

As the story unfolds, the impact of this absence extends beyond personal struggles, touching upon broader themes of resilience and self-discovery. The absent branch, rather than being a mere void, becomes a catalyst for forging an identity independent of traditional familial structures.

The emotional intricacies of growing up with an absent father offer insights into the resilience embedded within the human spirit. The quest for self-discovery and the forging of personal identity become a transformative journey, challenging preconceived notions and societal expectations.

In the process of recounting the complexities of an absent branch, the narrative also touches upon the universal theme of navigating family dynamics in the digital age. The emergence of technology as a means of communication introduces new dimensions to familial relationships, raising questions about the authenticity of connection in the absence of physical proximity.

The emotional nuances of the absent branch narrative unfold against the backdrop of evolving family structures and the shifting sands of societal expectations. As the narrative weaves through personal anecdotes, reflections, and societal observations, it invites readers to contemplate the multifaceted nature of family and the profound impact of an absent branch on the tapestry of one's life.

In writing about the absent branch, it brings a lot of emotions. Tears mix with the words as I try to capture the pain and longing. This story is not just about what happened; it's about the heartache that lingers.

As I finish these last paragraphs, the weight of the absent branch story is heavy. Every word digs into the soul, revealing the hurt that time couldn't mend. The yearning for a father's presence echoes through the lines, and the tears that fall silently speak of the emotional toll of growing up with an absent branch.

This story is a mix of love and pain, a testament to the complexity of family ties and the lasting impact of a missing father. By sharing this, I hope for understanding, closure, and the wish that the absent branch could one day find its place in the family tree.

The pen trembles over the paper, hesitant to dive into the deep emotions. The tears that fall hold the weight of unspoken words and unfulfilled wishes. In the midst of this emotional storm, there's a desire to stop, recognizing that some wounds stay tender and don't easily heal.

As the ink dries and the tears stop, the realization remains that the absent branch story is an ongoing journey with no clear end. By sharing these thoughts, there's a faint hope that the absent branch, though missing physically, might somehow find its place in the understanding, compassion, and eventual closure.

Chapter 4: Nurturing Seeds of Mentorship.

In the intricate dance of life, some relationships stand out as turning points, altering the course of one's narrative. As I reflect on my high school years, Mrs. Tsoai emerges as a central figure, weaving threads of mentorship and inspiration.

Mrs. Tsoai's impact reached beyond the boundaries of the classroom. Through her, I encountered the dynamic force that would become instrumental in shaping my journey.

One of the defining moments was the Youth Enterprise Society workshop in Welkom. Selected to represent my school, the experience was transformative. It was here that I began to understand the power of collaboration and community building. The seeds of partnership were sown, leading to the formation of a resilient team that defied expectations.

In 2018, as President of the Youth Enterprise Society, I navigated the complexities of leadership with the unwavering support of Mrs. Tsoai. Her guidance was a compass, steering me through challenges and victories alike. Together with my team, we not only represented our province but secured a remarkable place nationally, a testament to the strength forged through collaboration.

Amidst these triumphs, I met Basetsana Confidence Sheane, a force of inspiration. Together, we delved into the realms of oral presentation competitions, crafting a unique synergy that resonated with judges and audiences alike. From our first national competition to encounters with remarkable individuals, the journey was a tapestry woven with friendship, growth, and shared aspirations.

Mrs. Tsoai's involvement in my education extended beyond the confines of subjects taught. Her keen interest in my academic progress served as a compass, guiding me towards improvement and celebrating achievements. It was a relationship built on honesty and genuine concern, enriching my academic endeavors.

The seeds of friendship and collaboration planted during these formative years continue to bear fruit, shaping not only my academic pursuits but also influencing the trajectory of my personal growth.

Mrs. Tsoai's influence didn't stop at academics; it extended into the realm of public speaking and entrepreneurship. In 2019, we triumphed in the Eskom Simama Ranta Entrepreneural competition, marking another milestone. It was a testament to the courage and determination she instilled in me to lead the team to victory.

The partnership with Basetsana Confidence Sheane flourished under Mrs. Tsoai's mentorship. Together, we tackled different competitions, representing not just our school and province but embracing the opportunity to connect with young change-makers from diverse backgrounds. Through Basetsana, I found more than a teammate; she became a source of inspiration, a friend I looked up to despite the age difference.

Our journeys to places like Four Ways in Johannesburg, staying at the Indaba Hotel Spa and Conference Center, were not just adventures but moments of growth. Through these experiences, Mrs. Tsoai fostered an environment where learning extended beyond textbooks.

The invaluable support of Mrs. Tsoai became a catalyst for personal and professional growth. The collaboration between Basetsana and me became a dynamic force in competitions, with our names etched into the annals of achievements, fostering a legacy of triumphs.

Reflecting on these experiences, I see the chapters of my high school years as a testament to the seeds of friendship sown by Mrs. Tsoai. Her mentorship not only guided my academic journey but also nurtured partnerships and friendships that continue to flourish.

As I pen these thoughts, I can't help but express profound gratitude for the role Mrs. Tsoai played in shaping not just my high school narrative but laying the foundation for a future where collaboration, courage, and resilience intertwine to create stories yet to unfold.

Chapter 5: Who Am I?

I find myself navigating a complex web of emotions, often grappling with questions that linger in the quiet corners of my mind. Who am I? What defines the essence of my being?

I'm a boy, often misunderstood, erroneously labeled, and tangled in societal expectations. The whispers of speculation surround my identity, mistaking my nature for something it's not. A writer whose words resonate beyond the local echo, seeking solace in the universal embrace of understanding.

Yet, I tread cautiously, for the path of friendship is fraught with pitfalls. Many, quick to enter my life, are even quicker to exit. A disheartening dance of fleeting connections that leave me feeling adrift in a sea of isolation. Social platforms reflect a paradox – reactions in abundance, comments a rare commodity, a stark reminder of my ephemeral presence.

I harbor a sadness, an uninvited companion that shadows my steps. A solitude seeker, I find solace in the embrace of solitude, with only one steadfast friend echoing from the first chapter. Yet, this chapter isn't about him, but about unraveling the intricacies of my own existence.

The puzzle of fitting in eludes me, a perpetual outsider trying to navigate a world where I'm often made to feel inadequate. Acts of kindness met with swift forgetfulness, criticized for reasons unbeknownst to me, a perpetual cycle of being out of sync with the rhythm of societal expectations.

In this symphony of emotions, I grapple with the challenge of friendships that don't endure, partnerships that wane, and the haunting feeling of inadequacy that weaves through my thoughts. I yearn for connections that last, supporters who stand proud, and the acceptance that perfection is an illusion.

In the sanctuary of writing, I find respite. It's a mirror reflecting my true self, a cathartic escape from the shadows of depression and anxiety that linger relentlessly. Walking the streets, an exercise in self-consciousness, haunted by the phantom gaze of perceived judgment in crowded rooms.

Yet, amidst the struggle, I hold onto the lifeline that writing provides. An escape from the noise, a canvas to paint my inner world, and an opportunity to reshape my narrative. In the world's harshest realities, writing becomes the harbor of my emotions, the refuge of my thoughts.

In the labyrinth of self-discovery, I grapple with the echoes of forgotten friendships. It seems as if my social circle is defined by fleeting moments, a kaleidoscope of faces who vanish when life's journey becomes challenging. The ache of isolation settles deep within, yet amidst the void, writing stands as my steadfast companion. It listens to the unsaid, captures the nuances of my silence, and breathes life into the unspoken narratives.

Loneliness, a silent companion, whispers in the empty spaces of my soul. I yearn for genuine connections, for friendships that weather the storms of life. It's an elusive dream, an aspiration that flickers like a distant star in the night sky. Each attempt to forge bonds feels like navigating a maze where dead ends outnumber open pathways.

As I scroll through social media, I observe the vibrant tapestry of other lives, woven with camaraderie and shared joy. In contrast, my posts echo in the digital void, a silent testament to the hollowness that resonates in my offline world. The paradox of virtual connectivity and real-world solitude adds complexity to the narrative of who I am.

Every smile hides a reservoir of unshed tears, and beneath the laughter, there's a symphony of unspoken pain. It's a paradoxical existence, a delicate dance between presenting a façade to the world and confronting the vulnerability within. Writing becomes the bridge between these realms, allowing me to articulate the intricate dance of emotions in a language that transcends the boundaries of spoken words.

The world often appears as a stage where I play a role, scripted by societal expectations. Each performance leaves me yearning for authenticity, a space where I can shed the mask and simply be. Writing emerges as the sanctuary where pretense dissipates, and I can lay bare the complexities of my identity.

In the echoes of rejection, I grapple with the notion of self-worth. The incessant comparison to others, the perceived inadequacies, all contribute to a fractured sense of value. The narrative I pen becomes a mirror reflecting the strength woven into the very fabric of my being. It's an anthem of resilience, a declaration that my worth transcends the judgments of external eyes.

Navigating the intricacies of identity, I confront the stereotype of being misunderstood. It's a label that clings stubbornly, shaping interactions and coloring perceptions. Writing dismantles these misconceptions, revealing the depth beneath the surface, and inviting others to engage with the genuine essence of who I am.

Within the realm of emotions, there's a spectrum that spans from the brightest joy to the darkest despair. The written word acts as a compass, guiding me through this emotional landscape. It's a tool for introspection, a mirror reflecting the kaleidoscope of feelings that define the contours of my soul.

As I grapple with the complexities of mental health, writing becomes a therapeutic outlet. It's a dialogue with the shadows, an exploration of the inner recesses where anxiety and depression lurk. The pen, my ally, becomes an instrument of healing, transmuting pain into prose and navigating the labyrinth of emotions.

The journey of self-discovery extends beyond the individual, weaving connections to the broader world. Writing becomes a bridge to understanding, a lens through which I interpret the intricacies of societal dynamics. It's a call for empathy, an invitation to witness the human experience beyond the superficial veneer.

Beneath the layers of solitude, I harbor a longing for recognition, a desire to be seen and heard. Writing amplifies my voice, echoing in the vast expanse of digital spaces. It's a silent plea for acknowledgement, an attempt to carve out a niche where my narrative matters.

The societal expectation to conform to conventional norms casts a looming shadow over the landscape of self-expression. Writing becomes a rebellion, a refusal to be confined within the narrow boundaries dictated by societal norms. It's an assertion of individuality, a celebration of the unconventional.

In the tapestry of cultural identity, I grapple with the dichotomy of belonging and alienation. Writing serves as a bridge between worlds, allowing me to explore the nuances of cultural intricacies. It's an ode to the diverse facets that shape my identity, a celebration of the mosaic woven from the threads of heritage and personal experience.

At the intersection of dreams and reality, there's a tension that defines my aspirations. The gap between the envisioned future and the present moment is vast, and writing becomes the compass guiding me toward the realization of those dreams. It's an exploration of possibilities, a roadmap for the journey toward the desired destination.

Within the pages of my narrative, there's a recurring theme of resilience. Each setback, each moment of despair, becomes a catalyst for renewed determination. Writing captures the spirit of endurance, an anthem of defiance against the adversities that threaten to overshadow the path ahead.

In the quest for connection, I confront the paradox of intimacy and distance. The fear of vulnerability clashes with the innate human longing for genuine connection. Writing becomes the medium through which I navigate this delicate balance, forging connections through the art of storytelling.

As I reflect upon the tapestry of my existence, the recurring theme of faith emerges. It's not just a religious conviction but a belief in the inherent goodness that resides within the human spirit. Writing becomes a testament to this faith, an affirmation that, despite the shadows that may loom, there is an enduring light within that refuses to be extinguished.

Within the chapters of my life, there are moments of profound introspection, where the echoes of solitude are transformed into a symphony of self-discovery. Writing serves as the scribe, etching these moments into the annals of my personal history. It's a cathartic release, an unburdening of the soul that lays bare the vulnerabilities and triumphs.

The dichotomy of strength and fragility weaves its way into the narrative. Writing becomes the mirror reflecting the paradoxical nature of resilience coexisting with vulnerability. It's an acknowledgment that strength doesn't negate the fragility within; instead, they dance together in a delicate balance.

Amidst the shadows of self-doubt, the pen becomes a beacon of self-affirmation. It's a declaration that, despite the external judgments and internal uncertainties, there is an unshakeable core within that asserts its presence. Writing becomes a ritual of self-love, a celebration of the imperfect beauty inherent in my being.

In the realm of relationships, I grapple with the ephemeral nature of connections. Writing becomes the bridge that spans the chasm between hearts, allowing for the expression of sentiments that words spoken aloud may struggle to convey. It's a solace for the heart that seeks resonance in the vast expanse of human interactions.

The exploration of identity extends beyond the borders of personal narratives, delving into the societal constructs that shape perceptions. Writing becomes a tool for dismantling stereotypes, challenging preconceived notions, and advocating for a more inclusive understanding of diverse identities. It's a call for empathy and a celebration of the rich tapestry of human experiences.

The quest for recognition is not merely an external pursuit. It is an act of self-empowerment, a declaration that my worth is not contingent on the applause or recognition of others. In the solitude of my written words, I find a sanctuary where self-love blossoms, unaffected by the transient opinions of the world.

As I navigate the intricate dance of emotions, writing emerges as a trusted confidant. It absorbs the spectrum of feelings, from the euphoria of fleeting joys to the depths of profound sorrow. It's a therapeutic dialogue, a conversation with the self that transcends the limitations of spoken language.

In the mosaic of cultural identity, writing becomes a canvas where the hues of heritage and personal experience intertwine. It's an exploration of the nuances that shape my sense of belonging and the delicate balance between embracing tradition and forging a unique path. Through the written word, I articulate the complexities of cultural intersectionality.

The chapters of my narrative unfold against the backdrop of mental health struggles. Writing becomes a lifeline, offering solace in the midst of anxiety's tempest and the shadows of depression. It's an act of resilience, a testament to the transformative power of self-expression in navigating the labyrinth of emotional challenges.

Within the silent spaces of loneliness, writing serves as both companion and refuge. It transforms solitude from a burden into a creative haven where ideas bloom and introspection flourishes. The written word becomes a bridge to connect with the innermost recesses of my being, turning isolation into a contemplative sanctuary.

As I confront the societal pressures to conform, writing emerges as a rebellious act of individuality. It's an assertion of authenticity in a world that often demands conformity. The pen becomes a weapon against the constraints of societal norms, crafting a narrative that defies expectations and celebrates the uniqueness inherent in my identity.

The theme of resilience echoes throughout the narrative, manifesting in the face of setbacks and challenges. Writing captures the spirit of endurance, a defiant anthem that rises above the cacophony of adversity. Each word becomes a brushstroke painting the canvas of my journey with strokes of tenacity and unwavering determination.

In the exploration of dreams and aspirations, writing functions as both compass and chronicle. It maps the trajectory of envisioned futures, weaving a narrative that navigates the chasm between present reality and aspirations. The written word becomes a roadmap, guiding me toward the manifestation of my dreams.

Amidst the paradox of intimacy and distance in relationships, writing becomes the bridge that spans emotional landscapes. It's a means to articulate sentiments that linger in the unspoken spaces between hearts. Through the written word, connections are forged, and the intricate dance of human relationships finds expression.

The narrative also grapples with the yearning for recognition and acknowledgment. Writing becomes a voice that resonates in the digital expanse, a plea for visibility in a world where individual stories often fade into the background. It's an assertion that every narrative, no matter how singular, holds significance in the collective tapestry of human experiences.

In the symphony of emotions, faith emerges as a recurring motif. Writing becomes a testament to a profound belief, not just in religious conviction but in the innate goodness that resides within humanity. It's a declaration that, despite the shadows that may cast doubt, an enduring light persists within, illuminating the path forward.

As the chapters unfold, a recurrent theme is the dichotomy of strength and fragility. Writing becomes the mirror that reflects the coexistence of resilience and vulnerability. It's an acknowledgment that strength does not eradicate fragility but rather dances alongside it in a delicate balance, creating a nuanced portrait of the human spirit.

The exploration of identity transcends personal narratives to encompass societal constructs. Writing becomes a tool for dismantling stereotypes, challenging preconceived notions, and advocating for inclusivity. It's a call for empathy and a celebration of the rich tapestry of human experiences, reminding readers that every story contributes to the mosaic of collective understanding.

In the labyrinth of self-discovery, amidst the echoes of forgotten friendships and the solitude of self-exploration, writing stands as a pillar of strength. It's not just a means of expression but a journey of empowerment, resilience, and unwavering self-acceptance. Each word penned is a step toward a deeper understanding of who I am, a testament to the intricate tapestry of my existence, and an affirmation that, despite the challenges, I am Lebohang, embracing the complexity of my identity with courage and grace.

Chapter 6: The Ways We Live, We Love, and We Lie

In the early chapters of my life, love was a gentle melody, playing softly in the background of my childhood. Thato, a girl from my primary school days, colored my world with the innocence of youthful affection. Our connection was simple, yet it laid the foundation for the complex love stories that awaited me. Little did I know, the nuances of love were about to take center stage.

As life's chapters unfolded, I encountered different girls, each contributing a unique brushstroke to the canvas of my romantic journey. The first whispers of love also carried the sting of jealousy, a lesson learned from a friend who attempted to sabotage my connection with Thato. The complexities of rivalry and the fragility of early connections became evident, setting the stage for the intricate relationships that would follow.

High school brought its own set of challenges and heartbreaks. A significant chapter unfolded, where the intensity of a connection echoed through the hallways. Moments of genuine connection collided with unforeseen circumstances, teaching me about the importance of reciprocity and shared commitment in matters of the heart.

The tapestry of love continued to weave itself, introducing new characters with every turn of the page. Despite the challenges and heartbreaks, the desire for genuine connections persisted. A theme began to emerge—the importance of self-love. To love others authentically, I had to extend that love inward. The journey toward self-love became a crucial lesson before venturing into new relationships.

As I navigated the intricacies of relationships, the fear of repeating past mistakes loomed large. Contemplating parenthood and marriage stirred a mix of hope and caution. Each encounter served as a mirror reflecting lessons learned, guiding my steps toward greater self-awareness.

The chapter unfolds with the realization that love is an ongoing journey. Acknowledging past mistakes becomes a roadmap for navigating future connections with authenticity and vulnerability. While the tapestry may not capture every detail of each romantic encounter, it strives to convey the essence of my journey through love's labyrinth.

While the girls may not be explicitly named, their impact is woven into the fabric of my romantic experiences. Each girl played a unique role in shaping my narrative of love, contributing diverse hues to the canvas of my journey.

As the story continues, the quest for genuine connection and self-discovery remains at the forefront. The intricacies of love are examined through the lens of past experiences, offering valuable insights for the chapters yet to be written. In the grand tapestry of my life, love remains a central theme—a complex and multifaceted emotion that weaves its way through the fabric of my existence.

The girls, each contributing a unique hue to the canvas, symbolize the diverse shades of love that color my journey. This ongoing exploration of love, with its highs and lows, serves as a testament to the enduring human spirit in the ways we live, we love, and we lie.

As I reflect on the numerous chapters of love in my life, I recognize the importance of embracing vulnerability. Love's intricate dance involves stepping into the unknown, risking heartache for the chance of profound connection. Each encounter, whether fleeting or enduring, has shaped my capacity to love and be loved.

In the realm of romantic entanglements, the dichotomy between desire and restraint emerges as a recurring theme. The allure of passionate connection collides with the necessity of boundaries, presenting a delicate balance to navigate. Learning to set boundaries became a crucial aspect of preserving my emotional well-being and fostering healthier relationships.

Amidst the myriad emotions of love, the concept of self-love emerged as a guiding beacon. The realization that one must cultivate love within before sharing it with others became a transformative revelation. This journey toward self-love involves embracing imperfections, recognizing inherent worth, and dismantling the barriers that hinder genuine self-appreciation.

As the layers of my romantic narrative unfold, the influence of societal expectations and cultural nuances becomes increasingly apparent. Navigating love within the context of societal norms poses challenges, demanding introspection and a conscious effort to reconcile personal desires with external pressures. The evolving landscape of love reflects not only personal growth but also a shifting societal paradigm.

The ebb and flow of love's tide carry echoes of both joy and heartache. Each romantic interlude contributes to the evolving melody of my emotional symphony. The lessons learned from fleeting connections and enduring partnerships weave a rich tapestry of experiences, reinforcing the idea that love, in its myriad forms, remains an integral aspect of the human experience.

The exploration of love extends beyond romantic entanglements to encompass the broader spectrum of relationships. Friendships, familial bonds, and platonic connections contribute unique hues to the canvas of love. These diverse relationships, each with its own dynamics, offer a holistic view of the ways we live, we love, and we lie.

In the labyrinth of love, forgiveness emerges as a transformative force. The ability to forgive oneself and others becomes a crucial component of navigating the complexities of human connection. Grappling with the shadows of past mistakes, forgiveness becomes the key to unlocking the heart and allowing love to flourish anew. As I delve into the intricacies of forgiveness, I am confronted with the profound realization that healing is an essential aspect of the journey toward genuine connection.

The narrative of love expands beyond personal experiences to encompass the broader societal context. Examining the impact of cultural expectations on relationships reveals the intricate dance between tradition and personal autonomy. Navigating the intersection of cultural norms and individual desires adds another layer of complexity to the ongoing exploration of love.

As I stand at the crossroads of my romantic journey, the question of commitment echoes in the chambers of my heart. Delving into the depths of commitment involves a nuanced examination of loyalty, fidelity, and the delicate balance between autonomy and partnership. This exploration uncovers the evolving nature of commitment within the ever-changing landscape. Balancing the fiery passion that ignites romantic connections with the practical considerations of daily life requires a delicate choreography.

The chapters of love unfold with a nuanced exploration of how passion can coexist harmoniously with the realities of work, responsibilities, and shared goals. This intricate dance highlights the importance of finding synergy between the head and the heart in matters of the heart.

The passage of time becomes an ever-present character in the saga of love. As the clock ticks, relationships evolve, perspectives shift, and the essence of love transforms. The enduring nature of love becomes evident in its ability to weather the storms of change, adapting to the shifting sands of time.

And so, the chapter concludes, but the journey of love persists, with new pages waiting to be written, new characters waiting to make their entrance, and the perennial hope that the story of love will continue to evolve, enrich, and illuminate the chapters that lie ahead.

As I reflect on this intricate tapestry of love, I am reminded that the heart's journey is never linear. It's a symphony of emotions, a dance of vulnerability, and a canvas painted with the hues of joy, sorrow, and everything in between. The exploration of love is not a destination but an ongoing process of self-discovery, connection, and growth.

In the grand narrative of my life, love remains the central theme—a force that shapes, molds, and propels me forward. The girls, each contributing a unique brushstroke to the canvas, symbolize the diverse shades of love that color my journey. This ongoing exploration of love, with its highs and lows, serves as a testament to the enduring human spirit in the ways we live, we love, and we lie.

As I step into the unwritten chapters of my romantic journey, I carry with me the lessons learned, the scars healed, and the hope that love, in all its complexities, will continue to be the heartbeat of my existence. The chapters may vary in length and intensity, but the essence of love remains a constant, guiding me through the ever-changing landscapes of the heart.

In the intricate dance of love, I find solace, vulnerability becomes my strength, and the canvas of my life is adorned with the brushstrokes of genuine connection. The story of love unfolds not as a neatly scripted tale but as a beautifully chaotic masterpiece, where each chapter contributes to the evolving narrative of my heart.

And so, I embrace the uncertainty, savor the moments of joy, navigate the challenges with resilience, and continue to live, love, and perhaps lie—a complex symphony echoing the profound reality that in the ways we live, we love, and we lie, we discover the truest reflections of our souls.

Chapter 7: "Happiness is the Only Choice"

Some days I found myself navigating terrains that echoed with the absence of sandy shores and crashing waves. The metaphorical beach, a realm of calm and chaos, remained elusive, yet within the tumult of life's currents, I discovered the art of choosing happiness.

As the chapters unfolded, solitude became both a companion and a teacher. In the stillness of my own company, I unearthed the profound truth that happiness is not contingent upon external circumstances. Rather, it resides within the sanctuary of self-awareness and acceptance.

In the echoes of heartbreak and disappointment, I confronted the challenge of forging a path to happiness. The choice became clear—either succumb to the undertow of despair or rise above the waves with resilience and a steadfast commitment to joy.

A pivotal moment emerged in the form of a friend named Pontsho. Amidst life's tempests, his friendship was an anchor, a reminder that even in the absence of a literal beach, the shores of camaraderie could provide solace and laughter. Together, we navigated the complexities of existence, creating a haven where happiness thrived.

The dance with personal demons and shadows cast by insecurities became a central theme. Choosing happiness involved confronting those shadows, allowing vulnerability to coexist with strength, and embracing the imperfect symphony of my own humanity.

As I reflect upon the twists and turns of my narrative, I realize that the pursuit of happiness is not linear. It's a mosaic crafted from moments of triumph and tribulation. In the absence of a tranquil beach, I found happiness in the resilience that emerged from facing life's storms head-on.

The chapter of choosing happiness winds through the labyrinth of self-discovery. From the depths of self-reflection to the crescendo of shared laughter, it's a melody played on the strings of resilience, acceptance, and the unwavering belief that joy is a birthright.

Pontsho's impact on my journey is immeasurable. In his friendship, I found a confidant, a mirror reflecting the beauty in my flaws, and a co-author of moments where happiness became the prevailing theme. Through the ebb and flow of our camaraderie, I learned that the beach, in its metaphorical sense, exists wherever genuine connections are nurtured.

The tapestry of my life may lack the literal Imprints of sandy shores, but it's adorned with the footprints of resilience, laughter, and the conscious choice to embrace happiness. Each paragraph in this chapter unfolds as a testimony to the profound truth that happiness is not a destination—it's a continuous journey.

Solitude, with its contemplative silence, offered a canvas for introspection. In the absence of external distractions, I discovered the power of inner peace—a cornerstone in the construction of a life characterized by conscious happiness.

The scars of past wounds became not reminders of pain but testaments to the strength that arises from choosing happiness. Each scar narrates a story of survival, resilience, and the ability to find beauty even in the aftermath of life's tempests.

In the corridors of my own mind, I confronted the shadows that threatened to dim the light of happiness. It was a battle waged with self-compassion, acknowledging that the journey towards joy involves navigating through the complexities of one's own psyche.

Pontsho's friendship, like a lighthouse in the storm, illuminated the path to happiness. Whether in shared laughter or moments of vulnerability, his presence became a testament to the transformative power of authentic connections. In the absence of a literal beach, our camaraderie became the shore where happiness met the waves.

Even in the absence of a tranquil beach, I discovered that happiness is not contingent upon the external scenery. It's a state of being crafted through the intentional choices we make, the relationships we nurture, and the resilience we cultivate in the face of life's challenges.

The pursuit of happiness involves navigating the landscapes of joy and sorrow, basking in the warmth of shared moments, and finding solace in the sanctuary of self-love. In the vast tapestry of my experiences, the absence of a physical beach became inconsequential in the face of the profound realization that happiness, as a choice, transcends external landscapes.

This chapter weaves through the complexities of choosing happiness, embracing the nuances of human emotions, and acknowledging the significance of authentic connections. It stands as a testament to the belief that even in the absence of a literal beach, the shores of happiness can be found within the depths of self-awareness and genuine relationships.

As the chapter unfolds, it becomes evident that happiness is not a singular choice but a continuous series of decisions. Whether in solitude or in the company of kindred spirits, the beach of happiness manifests wherever the heart finds solace and joy.

In the grand tapestry of my journey, the absence of a literal beach became inconsequential in comparison to the myriad ways in which happiness manifested. From the stillness of introspection to the vivacity of shared laughter, each paragraph in this chapter echoes with the resounding truth that happiness is not just a choice—it's the only choice.

Chapter 8: The Grey Between Black and White

Amid the hushed hum of a Saturday evening, the clock inching toward 8 o'clock, my friend and I found ourselves drawn into a conversation that would unravel the intricacies of choice. The topic abruptly shifted to the ideological crossroads of capitalism and socialism. Pontsho, my friend, pressed for a clear-cut decision, a choice between the two. However, rather than succumb to the binary nature of the question, we embarked on a journey to explore the possibility of embracing both ideologies in different spheres of life. The realization dawned that life need not be confined to stark choices; the grey area between black and white could be a realm of harmony, where both systems coexist.

As we delved into the definitions of capitalism and socialism, Pontsho passionately argued for the merits of each system. Faced with the daunting decision, I hesitated, feeling the weight of choosing one over the other. Eventually, I opted for capitalism, drawn by its perceived benefits. However, the conversation took an unexpected turn when Pontsho revealed his intention to practice capitalism outside his family and socialism within, highlighting the fluidity of beliefs and challenging the notion of rigid choices.

The second Instance unfolded within the realm of coaching, where I found myself caught in the delicate web of selecting participants for a story-writing competition. Rather than pitting them against each other, I suggested an alternative path – collaboration. This decision, rooted in the belief that shared knowledge would yield better results, led to both participants securing national prizes in their respective age groups. The triumph of teamwork over competition became a testament to the boundless potential that emerges when we break free from binary choices.

A third scenario emerged when navigating advice from friends in different professions. Recognizing the unique value each friend brought, I purposefully avoided binary choices. Seeking guidance from a friend who's a medical doctor on health matters and turning to a law friend for ethical dilemmas exemplified the richness of varied perspectives. The chapter delves into the importance of avoiding rigid categorizations, showcasing how diverse inputs can lead to more nuanced decisions.

In essence, the chapter reflects on the idea that life offers a palette of choices beyond mere black and white. The instances discussed emphasize the importance of embracing the grey, acknowledging the potential for synergy in combining seemingly conflicting elements. Life, much like the intricate dance between capitalism and socialism, or the collaboration between competitors, thrives in the vibrant spectrum of choices. The journey through these diverse scenarios invites contemplation on the beauty that emerges when we navigate the grey areas of life.

Chapter 9: "Food for thought"

In the serene embrace of my parents' vacant room, I delved into the labyrinth of my own mind. This introspective odyssey unfolded as the intricate tapestry of my thoughts manifested, carving the unseen corridors of my inner world.

How frequently do our thoughts forge the barriers that bind us?

Amidst the silent musings, a friend extended an invitation to partake in the vibrant atmosphere of the Avenue – a social hub pulsating with life. The invitation prompted a dance of conflicting emotions within me, as I grappled with the question of venturing beyond the confines of my own contemplative haven.

He entered the room with a contagious enthusiasm, "Hey bro, how are you doing?" His eyes sparkled with excitement, eager to share the plans for the evening. I, on the other hand, lay there, lost in the tangle of my thoughts, hesitant about stepping into a world where every gaze felt like judgment.

My friend pressed on, "We're heading to the Avenue, are you coming?" I hesitated, feeling the weight of a thousand unseen eyes on me. "No, bro, I'm not going," I responded. The unspoken fear of judgment clung to my decision, as I believed the entire world would scrutinize my every move.

Reflecting on past chapters, I remembered expressing a sentiment – a haunting feeling that everyone avoided hanging out with me. Now, as I traced the contours of my thoughts, I began to unravel the intricate web woven by my mind, realizing the self-imposed isolation rooted in my perceptions.

It dawned on me that my thoughts were not merely musings but architects shaping the walls that confined me. The fear of being watched, the belief that others harbored ill feelings – these thoughts became the invisible chains stifling my ability to socialize and build meaningful connections.

As I recounted this conversation with my friend, I recognized the impact of my thoughts on my social dynamics. The Avenue, once a lively space teeming with potential connections, became a distant reality obscured by the barriers I unknowingly erected.

The deeper I delved into this introspective journey, the more I realized the power our thoughts wield in constructing the landscapes of our lives. The room, once a sanctuary for contemplation, morphed into a mental battleground where perceptions battled reality.

The unraveling thoughts painted a vivid picture of the complexity within, underscoring the need to challenge and reshape the narratives constructed by the mind. This chapter, a glimpse into the intricacies of thought, serves as a mirror reflecting the potential pitfalls and profound realizations borne out of the musings within.

In the ever-evolving saga of self-discovery, this exploration of thoughts marks a pivotal juncture. It invites contemplation on the threads that bind us, urging us to unravel the intricacies within, lest we become ensnared in the labyrinth of our own making.

As I conclude this chapter, the echoes of unraveling thoughts reverberate, leaving an indelible imprint on the narrative of my journey. The next chapter beckons, promising further revelations in the ongoing exploration of self and the intricate dance of thoughts that shape our existence.

Chapter 10: 10 Times Better

In the hallowed corridors of my high school, one name rang with a resonance that transcended mere academia — Mrs. Marais, a luminary in the realm of life sciences. Her teachings echoed the power of repetition, the transformative magic that unfolds when a concept is revisited ten times. Little did I fathom then that this principle would metamorphose into a guiding philosophy, weaving its intricate pattern through the fabric of my life's journey.

Life often unfolds as a series of beats, demanding not just a single note but a rhythmic dance of purposeful strides. Thus, the melody of "10 times better" became the anthem of my life, orchestrating a harmonious interplay of achievements, failures, and aspirations.

Academia, that measured arena where grades serve as the currency of understanding, taught me the art of perpetual ascent. What began as a mere climb from mediocrity evolved into a meticulous ascent from acceptable to adequate, from satisfying to the zenith of ambitions. The cadence of progress, it seemed, was composed of incremental steps.

Stepping onto the soccer field with dreams of rekindling my goalkeeping prowess, I committed to ten days of relentless practice. What transpired wasn't just a revelation of my limitations but a reaffirmation of the value in trying, failing, and trying again. Each attempt became a stepping stone, drawing me closer to comprehension, a testament to the transformative power of relentless perseverance.

In the realm of oratory, where words wield the magic of shaping destinies, the philosophy of doing things ten times better found its most resonant application. Speeches, once mere compositions, underwent a metamorphosis through repeated refinement. The tenfold scrutiny turned eloquence into a practiced art, making 2021 a year marked by the fruitful symphony of revisiting portfolios and speeches.

The annals of history are replete with tales of those who embraced the ethos of doing things ten times better. Thomas Edison, the luminary inventor of the light bulb, faced thousands of failures before witnessing the glow of success. J.K. Rowling confronted rejection from numerous publishers before the magic of Harry Potter enchanted the world.

As we navigate the symphony of life, let this chapter be more than an anthem; let it be a symphony of relentless refinement and unwavering commitment. Doing things ten times better isn't just a pursuit of excellence; it's a journey marked by the nuanced rhythm of repeated efforts. In every revisited word, perfected nuance, and tireless endeavor lies the symphony of progress.

Crucially, this journey of improvement isn't a solitary one. It's a collective endeavor, shared by those who dared to persist. Celebrities such as Oprah Winfrey, Michael Jordan, and Steven Spielberg faced setbacks and rejections before etching their names in the annals of history. Their stories echo the essence of this chapter — that each failed attempt is a brushstroke in the masterpiece of success.

So, dear reader, as you stand at the precipice of your dreams, I beckon you to heed the call to do things not just once, but ten times better. For in the echoes of effort multiplied, we uncover the symphony of our true potential. Onward, then, to the next crescendo, where the refrain of tenfold endeavors guides us toward greatness, turning every challenge into an opportunity for mastery.

Let the echoes of "10 times better" resonate not merely as words but as a guiding principle, an enduring anthem that propels us toward a future where every endeavor is etched with the indelible mark of relentless improvement. In the tapestry of life, the threads of effort, woven tenfold, create a narrative that transcends challenges, reaching toward the symphony of our full potential.

Epilogue

"Embarking on the journey of 'All That I Am' Part 1, we've explored the highs and lows, the victories, and the lessons. Through tales of resilience, self-discovery, and the pursuit of happiness, the pages have unfolded a myriad of experiences. As we close this chapter, remember that life's tapestry is woven with both challenges and triumphs. Every setback is an opportunity to rise, every fall a chance to stand taller. Embrace the uncharted paths, for they lead to self-discovery. So, fellow traveler, as we conclude this part, let the echoes of resilience reverberate in your heart, fueling the spirit to face the unwritten chapters with unwavering courage. Onward we march, for the best is yet to come."

All that I am...
Part II

Prologue

*A*s I sit here, no longer penning thoughts on a pad but facing the glowing screen of a laptop, I can't help but marvel at the journey behind and the path yet to unfold. Times have changed, and with them, so have I. Yet, the absence of a beard and the lingering echo of a squeaky voice are reminders that growth, much like this story, is a work in progress.

Ready to chronicle the second part of my life, I find myself in this moment of reflection, poised at the precipice of new adventures. The transition from the tangible pages to digital keystrokes signals not just an evolution in tools but a symbol of the maturity gained through the passages of time.

So, as we embark on this journey once more, it's not a farewell but a mere "until we meet again." And meet again, we shall.

Chapter 1: If I die tomorrow...do this

As I sit here, pen in hand, the weight of mortality presses upon me like a leaden cloak. Sickness has wrapped its icy fingers around my body, leaving me weakened and vulnerable. A sudden pain grips my chest, a sharp reminder of the fragility of life. And atop my head, a swollen lump throbs with the relentless pulse of infection, a cruel souvenir of a mosquito's venomous kiss.

In the stillness of the night, with only the dim glow of my bedside lamp to pierce the darkness, I find myself contemplating the unthinkable: what if I were to die tomorrow? What legacy would I leave behind? What words of wisdom would I impart to those who remain?

If I were to die tomorrow, let it be known that I have lived a life filled with passion and purpose. From the depths of despair to the heights of joy, I have embraced every moment with courage and conviction. My journey has been marked by triumphs and tribulations, but through it all, I have remained steadfast in my pursuit of truth and meaning.

If I were to die tomorrow, do not mourn for me, but celebrate the beauty of existence. For though my time on this earth may have been brief, I have left an indelible mark upon the hearts of those I have encountered. My spirit will linger in the laughter of loved ones, the kindness of strangers, and the whispers of nature's symphony.

If I were to die tomorrow, let my passing serve as a reminder of life's fragile beauty. Cherish each sunrise as if it were your last, savoring the warmth of its golden rays against your skin. Dance beneath the stars with reckless abandon, reveling in the boundless expanse of the universe.

If I were to die tomorrow, scatter my ashes upon the wind, releasing me to wander the farthest reaches of creation. Let me drift among the clouds, painting the sky with hues of gold and crimson. And when you gaze upon the horizon, know that I am there, a silent companion in the journey of life.

If I were to die tomorrow, do not weep for me, but rejoice in the knowledge that I have lived fully and loved deeply. Embrace each day with gratitude, for every sunrise is a gift, and every heartbeat a miracle. And remember, dear friend, that in the end, it is not the years in your life that matter, but the life in your years.

As I confront the specter of mortality, my thoughts turn to the ones I hold dear. If I were to die tomorrow, I would want them to know the depth of my love and the extent of my gratitude. To my family, I leave behind cherished memories of laughter and love, moments woven together like threads in the tapestry of time.

If I were to die tomorrow, I would want my loved ones to find solace in the knowledge that I am at peace. Death is not an end but a new beginning, a journey into the unknown. And though I may no longer walk beside them, my spirit will continue to guide and protect them from beyond the veil.

If I were to die tomorrow, let my legacy be one of kindness and compassion. In a world plagued by division and strife, let my memory serve as a beacon of hope, a reminder that we are all interconnected in the vast tapestry of existence. Let my life inspire others to reach out with open hearts and outstretched hands, bridging the gaps that separate us and forging bonds of friendship and understanding.

If I were to die tomorrow, let my passing be a call to action. Life is fleeting, and time is precious. Do not squander the moments you have been given, but seize each day with purpose and intention. Pursue your dreams with unwavering determination, for in the end, it is not the destination that matters, but the journey itself.

If I were to die tomorrow, I would want those left behind to know that I have no regrets. I have lived boldly and loved fiercely, embracing every opportunity that came my way. And though my time on this earth may have been short, it has been filled with moments of pure joy and unbridled laughter.

If I were to die tomorrow, let my life be a testament to the power of resilience and the triumph of the human spirit. I have faced adversity with courage and grace, rising from the ashes of defeat stronger and more determined than ever before. And though the road has been long and arduous, I have never lost sight of the light at the end of the tunnel.

If I were to die tomorrow, I would want my friends to know that they have enriched my life in ways I cannot begin to express. Each one has left an indelible mark upon my soul, shaping me into the person I am today. From late-night conversations to spontaneous adventures, every moment shared has been a gift beyond measure.

If I were to die tomorrow, I would want my friends to gather together and celebrate the beauty of life. Let them raise a glass in my honor, sharing stories and laughter long into the night. For though my physical presence may be gone, my spirit will live on in the memories we have created together.

If I were to die tomorrow, let my passing be a reminder to cherish the moments we have with one another. Life is fleeting, and tomorrow is never guaranteed. So let us make the most of the time we have, filling each day with love, laughter, and joy. And when the end finally comes, let us depart with no regrets, knowing that we have lived fully and loved deeply.

If I were to die tomorrow, I would want those who mourn my passing to find comfort in the knowledge that I am at peace. Death is not an end but a transition, a journey into the great unknown. And though my physical form may no longer walk among you, my spirit will continue to watch over and guide you from afar.

If I were to die tomorrow, let my memory be a source of inspiration and strength. Let my life serve as a reminder that even in the darkest of times, there is always hope. And though I may be gone, my legacy will endure, a beacon of light shining brightly in the darkness.

If I were to die tomorrow, let it be with a smile upon my lips and gratitude in my heart. For I have lived a life filled with love and laughter, and I am thankful for every moment, every experience, every breath. And though the journey may be over, the memories will live on, etched forever in the hearts of those I leave behind.

If I were to die tomorrow, let my passing be a celebration of life. Let there be no tears, no sorrow, but only joy for the time we shared together. And as you go forth into the world, remember me not with sadness but with a smile, knowing that I am at peace and that my love will always be with you.

If I were to die tomorrow, do not mourn for me, but celebrate the beauty of existence. For though my time on this earth may have been brief, I have left an indelible mark upon the hearts of those I have encountered. My spirit will linger in the laughter of loved ones, the kindness of strangers, and the whispers of nature's symphony.

If I were to die tomorrow, let my passing serve as a reminder of life's fragile beauty. Cherish each sunrise as if it were your last, savoring the warmth of its golden rays against your skin.

Chapter 2 : Awakening to Life's Fragile Beauty

I awaken to the sterile environment of a public hospital, the tang of disinfectant stinging my nostrils. My eyelids flutter open, greeted by the harsh glare of fluorescent lights overhead. As awareness floods back, I am struck by the realization that I have narrowly escaped the clutches of death.

In the aftermath of my near-fatal ordeal, lying prone amidst the clinical confines of the hospital room, I am filled with a profound sense of gratitude for the gift of life. Each shallow breath I draw is a testament to the delicate balance between existence and oblivion, a reminder of the fragility of human existence.

As the days pass, and I slowly regain my strength, I find myself reflecting on the events that brought me here. The suddenness of it all, the stark confrontation with mortality, leaves me humbled and awe-struck. It is a stark reminder that life is fleeting, that each moment is precious and irreplaceable.

Gazing out of the window at the world beyond, I am struck by the sheer beauty of existence. The sky stretches out before me, an endless expanse of azure punctuated by billowing clouds. The sun hangs low on the horizon, casting long shadows across the landscape. In that moment, I am filled with a profound sense of peace and serenity.

For in the midst of darkness, there is always light. In the depths of despair, there is always hope. Though my journey has been fraught with hardship and adversity, I am reminded that every challenge I have faced has served to strengthen my resolve.

As I am discharged from the hospital and return to the rhythm of everyday life, I carry with me a newfound appreciation for the beauty of existence. Life is too short to be spent in fear and regret, too precious to be squandered on trivial pursuits. Each day is a gift, a chance to embrace the wonders of the world and to live with purpose and passion.

In the quiet moments of reflection, as I contemplate the depths of my own mortality, I am filled with a sense of gratitude for the simple joys of life. The laughter of loved ones, the warmth of the sun on my skin, the gentle rustle of leaves in the wind – these are the moments that make life worth living.

And so, as I stand on the threshold of a new day, I vow to seize each moment with courage and conviction. For tomorrow is not promised to any of us, and the only way to truly honor the gift of life is to live it to the fullest.

As I step out into the world once more, I am struck by the vibrancy of life that surrounds me. The hustle and bustle of the city streets, the laughter of children playing in the park, the gentle hum of conversation in a crowded café – each moment is a testament to the resilience of the human spirit.

I find myself drawn to the simple pleasures of everyday life – the smell of freshly brewed coffee, the feel of cool grass beneath my feet, the sound of rain tapping against the windowpane. In these moments, I am reminded of the beauty that exists in the world, even in the midst of chaos and uncertainty.

As I continue on my journey, I am filled with a renewed sense of purpose and determination. No longer content to simply exist, I am determined to embrace life with open arms and an open heart. For in the end, it is not the years in our lives that matter, but the life in our years.

So I vow to live each day with intention and passion, to savor every moment and cherish every memory. For life is a precious gift, and it is up to each of us to make the most of it while we can.

Chapter 3: Still alive

As I sit here, pen in hand, reflecting on the harrowing experiences detailed in the preceding chapters, I am struck by the overwhelming sense of gratitude that washes over me. Despite the trials and tribulations, I am still alive – a testament to the resilience of the human spirit and the enduring power of hope.

In Chapter 1, aptly titled "If I die tomorrow...do this...", I recounted the visceral experience of confronting my own mortality. Faced with the looming specter of death, I was forced to reckon with the fragility of life and the preciousness of each passing moment. As I lay in that hospital bed, grappling with the uncertainty of what lay ahead, I made a silent vow to embrace every opportunity, to live each day as if it were my last.

Chapter 2, titled "Echoes of Solitude", delved into the depths of loneliness that often accompany the human experience. Despite being surrounded by a bustling metropolis and a myriad of digital connections, I found myself grappling with a profound sense of isolation. Yet, even in the darkest moments of solitude, I discovered a glimmer of hope – a flicker of light that illuminated the path forward.

As I reflect on these chapters, I am reminded of the resilience of the human spirit. In the face of adversity, we possess an innate capacity to endure, to overcome, and to thrive. It is a testament to the indomitable nature of the human soul – a force that transcends the confines of circumstance and adversity.

In the wake of my own trials and tribulations, I am filled with a renewed sense of purpose and determination. I refuse to be defined by the challenges that have come before me, but rather, I choose to embrace them as opportunities for growth and transformation.

With each passing day, I am reminded of the preciousness of life – a gift to be cherished and savored in all its complexity. And though the road ahead may be fraught with obstacles and uncertainties, I am filled with an unwavering sense of hope – a beacon that guides me through the darkness.

As I delve deeper into the recesses of my mind, I find myself grappling with the lingering echoes of solitude that pervaded Chapter 2. Loneliness, I have come to realize, is not merely a state of being, but rather a deeply ingrained facet of the human condition. It is a profound ache that resonates within the soul, a longing for connection that transcends the boundaries of space and time.

In the quiet moments of introspection, I find solace in the knowledge that I am not alone in my struggles. Across the vast tapestry of humanity, countless souls grapple with their own sense of isolation and yearning for belonging. It is a universal experience, one that unites us in our shared humanity and reminds us of our interconnectedness.

Yet, even in the depths of despair, there is a glimmer of hope – a small spark of light that pierces the darkness and illuminates the path forward. It is a reminder that, despite the challenges we face, we are never truly alone. There are always hands reaching out, hearts open to connection, and voices eager to be heard.

As I reflect on the trials and tribulations of the past, I am struck by the resilience of the human spirit. Time and time again, we find the strength to persevere, to rise above the ashes of despair, and to forge a new path forward. It is a testament to the boundless capacity of the human heart – a wellspring of courage and resilience that knows no bounds.

In the face of adversity, we are called to embrace the full spectrum of human emotion – from the depths of despair to the heights of joy. It is through this embrace that we find our truest selves, our most authentic expression of humanity. And it is in this space of vulnerability that we discover the power of connection – the transformative force that binds us together as one.

As I look to the future, I am filled with a sense of cautious optimism. Though the road ahead may be fraught with challenges, I know that I do not walk it alone. With each step forward, I am buoyed by the support of loved ones, the wisdom of mentors, and the resilience of the human spirit.

And so, I embrace the journey with an open heart and a steadfast determination. For though the path may be uncertain, I am guided by the unwavering belief that, in the end, love will always prevail.

Chapter 4: I think...

In the quiet moments of solitude, I find myself lost in thought, pondering the myriad possibilities that lie ahead. With each passing day, my mind drifts to the lofty aspirations that have taken root within my heart – dreams of greatness, of leaving an indelible mark upon the world.

As I gaze out into the vast expanse of the universe, I am filled with a sense of awe and wonder. How small we are, mere specks of dust adrift in the cosmic sea, and yet how boundless our potential. In the grand tapestry of existence, each of us holds within us the power to shape our own destiny.

It Is this realization that fuels my ambition, igniting a fire within me to reach for the stars and chase after my dreams with unwavering determination. For I refuse to be confined by the limitations of the status quo – I yearn for something more, something extraordinary.

I dream of penning words that will resonate with hearts across the globe, of crafting stories that will stand the test of time and inspire generations yet unborn. With each stroke of the keyboard, I am one step closer to realizing this vision, one word closer to making my mark upon the world.

But dreams alone are not enough – they must be tempered with action, fueled by perseverance and unwavering resolve. And so, I commit myself wholeheartedly to the pursuit of my passions, to honing my craft and perfecting my art with every fiber of my being.

In the face of adversity, I remain undaunted, for I know that every setback is but a stepping stone on the path to greatness. With each challenge that I overcome, I grow stronger, more resilient, more determined than ever to see my dreams through to fruition.

And so, I press on, driven by a relentless hunger for success and a steadfast belief in my own abilities. For I know that within me lies the potential to achieve greatness, to leave a lasting legacy that will endure long after I am gone.

In the solitude of my thoughts, I find solace amidst the chaos of the world. It is here, in the quiet moments of introspection, that I am able to truly connect with myself and explore the depths of my innermost desires.

As I delve deeper into the recesses of my mind, I am confronted with a myriad of emotions – fear, doubt, uncertainty – all vying for my attention. And yet, amidst the turmoil, there is a glimmer of hope, a beacon of light that guides me through the darkness.

For within me lies an unyielding determination, a fierce resolve to overcome whatever obstacles may stand in my way. With each passing day, I am reminded of the boundless potential that resides within me, waiting to be unleashed upon the world.

It is this realization that fuels my dreams, driving me ever forward on the path to greatness. For I refuse to be confined by the limitations of my circumstances – I am destined for something greater, something beyond the ordinary.

With each passing moment, I feel myself drawing closer to my goals, inching ever closer to the realization of my dreams. And though the journey may be long and arduous, I am undeterred. For I know that with perseverance and determination, anything is possible.

As I look out upon the world, I am filled with a sense of wonder and awe. The possibilities are endless, and I am eager to explore every avenue that life has to offer. From the highest peaks to the deepest valleys, I am ready to embrace whatever challenges may come my way.

But even amidst the hustle and bustle of daily life, I find moments of stillness and tranquility. It is in these moments that I am able to reflect on the journey that has brought me to this point, to appreciate the struggles and triumphs that have shaped me into the person I am today.

And though the road ahead may be uncertain, I am filled with a sense of optimism and excitement for the future. For I know that with each passing day, I am one step closer to realizing my dreams and fulfilling my destiny.

As I stand on the precipice of greatness, I am filled with a renewed sense of purpose and determination. I am ready to face whatever challenges may come my way, confident in my ability to overcome any obstacle that stands in my path.

For I know that within me lies the power to achieve greatness, to leave a lasting impact upon the world. And so, I press on, fueled by the fire of my dreams and the unwavering belief that anything is possible.

In the end, it is not the destination that matters, but the journey itself. So I dream on, my aspirations lighting the way like beacons in the night. For I am determined to carve out a place for myself in the annals of history, to make my mark upon the world and leave a legacy that will inspire others to follow in my footsteps.

Chapter 5: If I wasn't born a writer...

I often find myself pondering what life would be like if I hadn't been born a writer. Would I still possess the same passion for words, the same desire to share my thoughts and experiences with the world?

Without the gift of writing, I imagine that I would have found another outlet for self-expression. Perhaps I would have turned to music, using melodies and lyrics to convey the depth of my emotions. Or maybe I would have pursued a career in the visual arts, channeling my creativity into paintings or sculptures that spoke volumes without uttering a single word.

But no matter the medium, one thing is certain – I would still be driven by a burning desire to make my mark on the world, to leave behind a legacy that would endure long after I am gone. For at the core of my being lies a relentless drive to create, to inspire, to make a difference in the lives of others.

Without the written word to guide me, I would undoubtedly face a different set of challenges and obstacles along my journey. But I am confident that I would rise to meet them with the same resilience and determination that has carried me through countless trials and tribulations in the past.

For creativity knows no bounds, and the human spirit is infinitely adaptable. Even in the absence of writing, I would find a way to channel my innermost thoughts and feelings, to share them with the world in whatever form they may take.

As I delve deeper into the realm of imagination, I cannot help but wonder how different my life would be if I had not been born a writer. Would I still possess the same insatiable curiosity, the same relentless drive to explore the depths of human experience?

Without the written word to guide me, I imagine that I would have pursued a different path in life. Perhaps I would have been drawn to the sciences, seeking to unravel the mysteries of the universe through empirical observation and experimentation. Or maybe I would have been drawn to the world of business, eager to carve out my own niche in the competitive marketplace.

But no matter the direction my life may have taken, one thing is certain – I would still be driven by a thirst for knowledge, a hunger to understand the world around me. For even in the absence of writing, the quest for truth and understanding remains a fundamental aspect of the human condition.

Without the outlet of writing to express myself, I would undoubtedly have found other ways to channel my creativity. Perhaps I would have turned to music, using melodies and harmonies to convey the depth of my emotions. Or maybe I would have explored the visual arts, creating paintings and sculptures that spoke volumes without uttering a single word.

But even as I contemplate these alternate paths, I cannot shake the feeling that writing is an integral part of who I am. It is woven into the very fabric of my being, shaping my thoughts and actions in ways that are both profound and ineffable.

For me, writing is more than just a means of communication – it is a lifeline, a way of navigating the tumultuous waters of existence. It is through writing that I am able to make sense of the world, to distill the chaos and confusion into something meaningful and coherent.

And so, as I reflect on what it means to be a writer, I am filled with a profound sense of gratitude. Gratitude for the gift of language, for the power of words to illuminate the darkest corners of the human psyche. Gratitude for the opportunity to share my thoughts and experiences with others, to forge connections that transcend time and space.

In the end, whether I was born a writer or not is beside the point. What matters is that I have found my calling, my purpose in life. And for that, I am eternally grateful.

And so, as I continue on my journey as a writer, I am grateful for the gift that has been bestowed upon me. It is a privilege and a responsibility, one that I do not take lightly. For with each word I write, I am able to touch the lives of others, to inspire, to provoke thought, to spark change.

So whether I was born a writer or not, I know that my purpose remains the same – to use my voice to make a difference in the world, to leave behind a legacy that will endure for generations to come. And for that, I am eternally grateful.

Chapter 6: Success not suck-sess...

I find myself caught in a perpetual cycle of ambition and achievement. It is a journey fraught with challenges and obstacles, yet I press on, driven by an insatiable desire to reach ever greater heights.

But as I reflect on what it means to be successful, I cannot help but wonder – am I chasing the right dream? Am I truly striving for success, or am I merely chasing after the hollow trappings of wealth and fame?

In the modern world, success is often equated with material wealth and status. We measure our worth by the size of our bank accounts, the prestige of our job titles, the number of followers on social media. But is this truly success, or is it merely a shallow imitation of the real thing?

For me, success is not just about achieving external markers of achievement. It is about living a life of purpose and fulfillment, about making a positive impact on the world around me. It is about finding joy and meaning in the journey itself, rather than fixating solely on the destination.

In my quest for success, I have come to realize that true fulfillment lies not in the accumulation of wealth or status, but in the pursuit of passions and interests that bring joy and fulfillment. It is about following my heart and staying true to myself, even in the face of adversity and criticism.

But success is not always easy to define or attain. It requires dedication, perseverance, and a willingness to embrace failure as an opportunity for growth. It is about learning from setbacks and using them as stepping stones to future success.

As I navigate the complexities of the modern world, I am reminded that success is not a destination, but a journey. It is about constantly striving to be the best version of myself, both personally and professionally. It is about embracing the challenges and opportunities that come my way, and using them to propel myself forward on the path to success.

In the end, whether I achieve the external markers of success is secondary to the sense of fulfillment and purpose that I derive from the journey itself. For true success lies not in what we accomplish, but in who we become along the way.

Chapter 7: A Day in the Life

As the first light of dawn breaks through the curtains, I awaken to a new day. With a heavy heart and a nagging pain in my chest from a mosquito bite, I rise to greet the morning. Each day is a gift, and I embrace it with gratitude.

After opening my eyes, I take a moment to reflect on the day ahead, contemplating the tasks and challenges awaiting me. Despite the uncertainty, I find solace in the routine that lies ahead.

The first order of business is breakfast. I prepare a simple meal to fuel my body for the day ahead, ensuring that I take my medication to ease the discomfort in my chest. With each bite, I am reminded of the fragility of life and the importance of cherishing each moment.

Once nourished, I turn my attention to household chores. Whether it's tidying up my own space or helping out at my mother's house, I find satisfaction in creating a clean and organized environment.

As I go about my tasks, I find myself drawn to the soothing sounds of music. I curate playlists for each day of the week, selecting songs that reflect my mood and inspire my creativity. Whether it's the soulful melodies of The Weeknd, the catchy tunes of Justin Bieber, the eclectic beats of Goldfish, or the vibrant rhythms of Crazy White Boy, music has a way of setting the tone for my day.

In addition to mainstream music, I also find inspiration in Afro Gospel, drawing influence from artists like Tasha Cobbs and other Black American giants. In the South African atmosphere, Joyous Celebration and Spirit of Praise play a significant role in my playlist, offering a sense of liberation and spiritual growth.

With music as my companion, I dive into my work. As a reporter, I am tasked with covering a range of topics, from sports and recreation to crime and lifestyle. Each article is an opportunity to share stories and connect with readers, and I approach my work with diligence and passion.

In between assignments, I make time for poetry. Writing has always been my true passion, and I find solace in the rhythm of words and the power of expression. Whether penning verses of joy or exploring the depths of sorrow, poetry is my sanctuary.

But amidst the hustle and bustle of daily life, I also make time for self-reflection. I recognize the importance of nurturing my mind, body, and soul, and I strive to find moments of peace and tranquility amidst the chaos.

In the evenings, I seek refuge in the quiet corners of the library, immersing myself in the world of literature and ideas. Here, surrounded by books and knowledge, I find inspiration and renewal.

As the day draws to a close, I return home, weary but content. I take comfort in the familiar rituals of the evening – a hot meal, a favorite television show, and the embrace of loved ones.

In the midst of it all, I am grateful for the love and support of my girlfriend, who brings joy and companionship to my life. She is my rock, my confidante, and my biggest cheerleader.

Inspired by literary giants like William Shakespeare and Maya Angelou, as well as contemporary artists like The Weeknd and Justin Bieber, I aspire to leave my mark on the world through my writing. Their words and music have shaped my worldview and fueled my passion for storytelling.

And as the day comes to an end, I am reminded of the simple joys that make life worth living. Tomorrow is uncertain, but today is a gift – and I intend to cherish it always.

Chapter 8: Random-encounter

During our bus ride to the National Heritage Council event I adjudicated, I found myself seated next to a lively individual named Kgosana Moeketsi. As we struck up a conversation, I quickly realized that Kgosana possessed a keen interest in entrepreneurship. He shared stories of his own ventures and experiences, offering valuable insights into the world of business.

Kgosana's enthusiasm for entrepreneurship was infectious, and I found myself drawn into his world of ideas and possibilities. He spoke passionately about the importance of innovation and creativity in business, emphasizing the need to constantly adapt and evolve in order to succeed.

As our journey continued, Kgosana regaled me with tales of his various business ventures, from starting his own e-commerce store to investing in real estate. His entrepreneurial spirit was palpable, and I couldn't help but be inspired by his drive and determination.

I listened intently as Kgosana shared his strategies for success, emphasizing the importance of networking and building strong relationships within the business community. He stressed the value of collaboration and encouraged me to seek out mentors who could offer guidance and support on my own entrepreneurial journey.

As Kgosana spoke, I found myself nodding along in agreement, eager to apply his advice to my own endeavors. He spoke with such confidence and conviction that I couldn't help but feel empowered and motivated to take action.

Throughout our conversation, Kgosana emphasized the importance of resilience and perseverance in the face of challenges. He shared stories of setbacks and failures he had encountered along the way, but also spoke of the valuable lessons he had learned from these experiences.

I realized that entrepreneurship was not just about making money; it was about pursuing your passions and creating something meaningful. Kgosana's story reminded me that success in business comes from following your instincts, taking calculated risks, and never being afraid to fail.

As the bus journey came to an end, I felt a renewed sense of purpose and excitement about my own entrepreneurial journey. Thanks to Kgosana's insights and inspiration, I was ready to take on new challenges and pursue my dreams with confidence and determination.

Walking away from our conversation, I couldn't help but feel grateful for the chance encounter with Kgosana. His words had sparked a fire within me, igniting a newfound passion for entrepreneurship and a determination to succeed.

Reflecting on our discussion, I realized that entrepreneurship was not just a career path; it was a mindset. It was about approaching life with curiosity, creativity, and a willingness to embrace change and uncertainty.

As I boarded the bus, I made a mental note to reach out to Kgosana in the future, eager to continue our conversation and learn more from his experiences. I knew that his guidance and mentorship would be invaluable as I navigated the challenges of entrepreneurship.

As the bus pulled away from the curb, I couldn't help but feel a sense of excitement and anticipation for the journey ahead. With Kgosana's words echoing in my mind, I felt ready to embrace the challenges and opportunities that lay before me, confident in my ability to succeed as an entrepreneur.

Chapter 10: When lives throws a curb...

In life, we often encounter unexpected challenges and obstacles that can leave us feeling discouraged and defeated. But it's how we choose to respond to these challenges that ultimately defines us. This chapter explores the concept of resilience and the power of turning adversity into opportunity.

One of the most valuable lessons I've learned is that when life gives you lemons, you have the choice to either succumb to despair or to make lemonade. This age-old adage reminds us that even in the face of adversity, there is always an opportunity to find a silver lining.

Throughout my own journey, I've encountered numerous setbacks and obstacles that have tested my resolve and determination. From personal struggles to professional setbacks, I've faced my fair share of challenges. But each time life threw me a curveball, I made a conscious decision to rise above it and turn adversity into opportunity.

One of the most memorable experiences that taught me the importance of resilience was when I faced a major setback in my career. Despite pouring my heart and soul into a project, it ultimately failed to materialize, leaving me feeling defeated and disillusioned. But instead of dwelling on my misfortune, I chose to view it as a learning opportunity.

I took stock of the lessons I had learned from the experience and used them to fuel my determination to succeed. Rather than allowing myself to be consumed by negativity, I channeled my energy into exploring new opportunities and pursuing my passions with renewed vigor.

In hindsight, I realize that the setback I faced was a blessing in disguise. It forced me to reevaluate my priorities and rediscover what truly mattered to me. It also taught me the importance of resilience and perseverance in the face of adversity.

Looking back on that experience, I'm grateful for the valuable lessons it taught me and the person it helped me become. It's a reminder that even in our darkest moments, there is always a glimmer of hope and opportunity waiting to be discovered.

In 2023, I embarked on a journey to write my first ever novel titled "Falling." It was meant to be a South African romance, filled with passion, intrigue, and heartwarming moments. However, what started as a labor of love quickly turned into a trial by fire.

As I poured my heart and soul into crafting the story, I encountered countless challenges along the way. From writer's block to self-doubt, I struggled to find my voice and bring my vision to life on the page. But despite the obstacles, I persevered, fueled by a burning desire to share my story with the world.

When the novel was finally completed, I eagerly sent it off to publishers and awaited their feedback. However, the response I received was not what I had hoped for. Instead of praise and adoration, my manuscript was met with criticism and rejection.

Critics questioned my credibility as a writer, citing flaws in the plot, character development, and prose. Some even went as far as to suggest that I should abandon my dreams of becoming a novelist altogether. It was a devastating blow to my confidence and self-esteem.

But instead of allowing myself to be consumed by despair, I chose to view the experience as a learning opportunity. I took stock of the feedback I had received and used it to identify areas for improvement. Rather than giving up on my dreams, I doubled down on my commitment to honing my craft and becoming a better writer.

With each rejection, I grew stronger and more determined to succeed. I poured myself into my work, dedicating countless hours to studying the craft of writing and refining my skills. Slowly but surely, I began to see progress, and my passion for storytelling was reignited.

Eventually, after months of hard work and perseverance, I emerged from the ashes of failure with a newfound sense of purpose and determination. I had transformed my setback into an opportunity for growth and self-discovery. And while "Falling" may not have been the success I had hoped for, it was the catalyst for a much greater journey.

Today, as I reflect on that challenging chapter of my life, I'm grateful for the lessons it taught me and the person it helped me become. It's a reminder that failure is not the end of the road, but rather a stepping stone on the path to success. And who knows? Perhaps one day, I'll revisit "Falling" and turn it into the masterpiece I always knew it could be. Until then, I'll continue to chase my dreams and write my own story, one page at a time.

So the next time life throws you a curveball, remember that you have the power to choose how you respond. Instead of allowing yourself to be overcome by despair, embrace the challenge and look for ways to turn it into an opportunity. Who knows? You might just end up making the best lemonade you've ever tasted.

Epilogue:

As I pen down these final words, I'm struck by the journey I've undertaken, the highs and lows, the triumphs and tribulations. This book is a reflection of who I am, a snapshot of the thoughts and experiences that have shaped me thus far. But it is not the end of my story.

From the introspective musings of Chapter 1 to the trials and triumphs chronicled in each subsequent chapter, I've laid bare my innermost thoughts and emotions. Every word, every sentence, is a testament to the person I am today.

But just as the final chapter draws to a close, so too does this part of my life. It's not the end, but rather a new beginning, a chance to write the next chapter in my story. Though weary and still feeling the ache in my chest, I dream of a tomorrow filled with excitement and possibility.

So as I bid farewell to this book and the words contained within, I do so with a sense of gratitude and anticipation for what lies ahead. Tired as I may be, I look forward to the adventures that await me. Until then, deuces.

Did you love *Thoughts: All that I am...?* Then you should read *Mohlolo : In the shadows of hope.*[1] by Lebohang Xavier Poetry!

[2]

Mohlolo : In the shadows of hope is a captivating and heartwarming tale that follows the remarkable life journey of Mohlolo, a young orphan who defies the odds and discovers the transformative power of love, friendship, and the indomitable human spirit.

From the early days of loss and longing in St. Louis Children's Home to the challenges and triumphs of adulthood, Mohlolo's story is a testament to resilience, perseverance, and the unwavering bonds of friendship.

---

1. https://books2read.com/u/38WwPL

2. https://books2read.com/u/38WwPL

As Mohlolo navigates the complexities of his upbringing and the search for belonging, he encounters a cast of unforgettable characters who leave an indelible mark on his life. From the nurturing and compassionate cook, MaMokoena, who becomes a surrogate mother, to his childhood friend Pontsho, who stands by his side through thick and thin, each person contributes to his growth and development.

Through the pages of this book, readers are transported into the vibrant landscapes of South Africa, where they witness the joys and sorrows, hopes and dreams that shape Mohlolo's journey. From the dusty streets of the township to the halls of the prestigious Taiwe Secondary School, and eventually to the challenges and triumphs of adulthood, the story unfolds with authenticity, depth, and a profound sense of humanity.

Mohlolo: In the shadows of hope explores universal themes of love, loss, identity, and the power of human connection. It delves into the complexities of family, the struggles of personal growth, and the resilience of the human spirit in the face of adversity. It is a story that inspires, challenges, and reminds us of the strength we possess within ourselves and the transformative power of the relationships we forge along the way.

Through beautifully crafted prose and vivid storytelling, the author invites readers to reflect on their own lives, to embrace the power of love, and to find hope in even the darkest of circumstances. With each turn of the page, readers will be captivated by Mohlolo's journey, rooting for his triumphs, empathizing with his struggles, and ultimately celebrating the enduring power of love and resilience.

Mohlolo: In the shadows of hope is a poignant and uplifting narrative that resonates long after the final page is turned. It serves as a reminder that no matter the challenges we face, the connections we form and the love we cultivate have the power to heal, transform, and guide us towards a future filled with hope, joy, and the boundless possibilities of the human spirit.

Join Mohlolo on his extraordinary journey as he discovers the true meaning of family, the strength of the human heart, and the profound impact of love in shaping our lives.

Also by Lebohang Xavier Poetry

Mohlolo
Mohlolo: In the Shadows of Hope

Thoughts
Thoughts: All that I am...

Standalone
Mohlolo : In the shadows of hope.
Mohlolo: In the Shadows of hope.
Falling

Also by Lebohang Phoshuli

Mohlolo
Mohlolo: In the Shadows of Hope

Thoughts
Thoughts: All that I am...

Standalone
Falling

About the Author

Lebohang Phoshudi, born and bred in Theunissen on 02 March, is an aspiring author with a passion for storytelling. Growing up in a small town, Lebohang developed a deep appreciation for literature and the power of words to transport readers to different worlds.

From a young age, Lebohang was captivated by books and spent countless hours immersed in various genres, ranging from fantasy and science fiction to historical fiction and contemporary literature. This early love for reading sparked a desire to create original stories and share them with others.

Lebohang's writing journey began in high school when they started penning short stories and poems. These early attempts at storytelling allowed them to explore different writing styles and experiment with narrative techniques.

Lebohang also participated in writing workshops and joined local writing groups, connecting with fellow aspiring authors and learning from experienced writers. These interactions allowed them to receive valuable feedback, hone their writing abilities, and gain confidence in their unique voice.

Lebohang's writing style is characterized by vivid descriptions, compelling characters, and thought-provoking themes. They strive to create stories that resonate with readers, exploring universal emotions and experiences while also challenging societal norms and perceptions.

As an aspiring author, Lebohang dreams of publishing their own novel someday, hoping to transport readers to new worlds and provoke thought through their writing. They draw inspiration from a wide range of sources, including nature, personal experiences, and the diverse cultures and traditions they encountered growing up in Theunissen.

In addition to their passion for fiction, Lebohang is also keen on exploring non-fiction writing, particularly in the areas of social issues, personal development, and cultural exploration. They believe that writing has the power to educate, inspire, and foster empathy, and they aspire to contribute to these endeavors.

Lebohang Phoshudi's journey as an aspiring author is driven by a profound love for storytelling and a commitment to crafting narratives that entertain, enlighten, and provoke thought. With their talent, dedication, and determination, they are poised to make their mark on the literary world and captivate readers with their unique stories.